I0572080

Aïschah Silver Moon

Aïschah Silver Moon

LANGUAGE OF THE STARS

Alain Louis Camus

ALAIN FRANÇOIS

Contents

DEDICATION AND ACKNOWLEDGEMENT

Alice Camus
My great grandmother
Inspiration for the character Aïschah.

Front cover photograph
Benjamin Voros
(Unsplash)

'Star Map'
Design: © Alain Francois

This book is a work of fiction. Names, characters, places, and incidents are the product of the author's imagination or are used fictitiously. Any resemblance to actual events, religions, locales, or persons, living or dead, is coincidental.

This right of Alain François (Alain Louis Camus – nom de plume), to be identified as the Author of the Work has been asserted in accordance with the Copyright, Designs and Patents Act 1988.

All Rights Reserved. No part of this publication may be reproduced, scanned, stored in a retrieval system, or transmitted, in any form or by any means without the prior written permission of the publisher, nor be otherwise circulate in any form of binding or cover other than that in which it is published and without a similar condition being imposed on the subsequent purchaser.

No part of this publication may be scanned, or input into an AI system.

Copyright © 2024 Alain Jean Francois

(Alain Louis Camus – nom de plume)

ISBN paperback 978-0-6457676-4-3

First Printing, 2024

The star map was done. At first glance it seemed complex, filled with shapes, lines, runic symbols, numbers, and numerous side notes; all handwritten in Aïschah's elegant style.

When Aïschah finally looked at her handy work, she realised that she had less than twenty years to accomplish her life's work.

If the child is talented, it will take less than that, she thought.

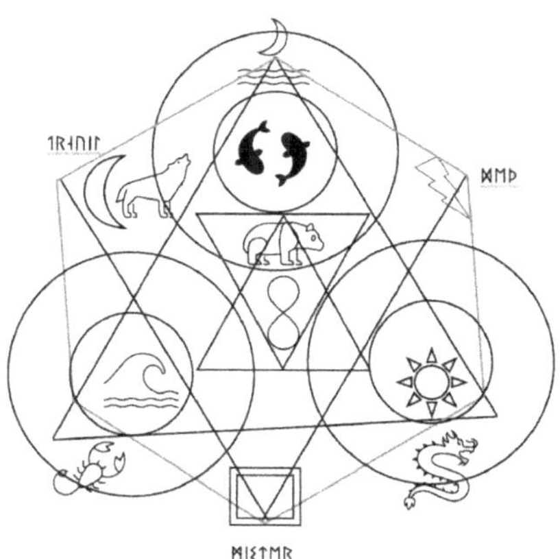

1

✋

Celeste, or Caelesti, meaning 'of the sky', as she was known in her hometown, woke up with a start. Intent on remembering the dream she just had, her eyes drifted to the small window in their house. Thick woolly clouds drifted by and slowly, eventually caught at the top of the Asfaine mountains, hung there like fat sheep on their slopes. She could hear her husband's soft breathing next to her. Haakon was still fast asleep.

Closing her eyes, she focussed on the images that were starting to fade. *Blue, the colour was blue and there was a lot of it;* she thought. The face of a young boy had emerged from a blue ocean. *It is the ocean of Malkizar,* a small voice stated in her mind. Her heart quickened at the memory. He had stark black hair and blue eyes. A solemn look on his face but then gave such a smile that almost made her cry. This was the third time she had experienced this dream. *I should go and speak with Aïschah,* she thought. She gave a small wince, her husband Haakon, wasn't very keen on her being seen with Aïschah.

Shortly after their marriage in her hometown, they had moved to the Asfaine mountains. They moved into Haakon's house. Although still young, as chief, his house was at the end of the village and a little grander than the others. Aïschah was the first person Celeste had met and had welcomed her. Celeste had heard the village rumours, that Aïschah was a witch, that she also had medicinal knowledge that could cure any illness. Haakon felt he had a reputation to uphold and was opposed to what he termed 'the old ways.' Celeste understood that he meant magic, the practice of the arts of healing and seership. While not strictly opposed to the art of healing, his understanding of herbal medicine was basic and limited to what his own mother had imparted to him in his youth.

When they had arrived, Aïschah had welcomed them and somehow paid a particular interest in Celeste and her welfare. She had offered once or twice to teach her basic herbal remedies. Haakon reluctantly agreed, seeing that it would benefit him and his family if ever they fell ill. It meant that he could avoid having to be seen consulting Aïschah. Although she was considered a powerful seer and one of the Elders of the Council of Magicians and had often made predictions that turned out to be accurate, he had never felt comfortable with her.

Celeste stretched and turned her head toward Haakon's sleeping form. Seeing his unshaved masculine face, his brows slightly knitted as if considering a complex issue in his sleep, she smiled knowing that he loved her beyond measure. He would not object to her going to Aïschah, he would just be concerned for her welfare and reputation.

Gently, so as not to disturb him, she rose, making sure the covers would not fall off him. She shivered slightly as her feet touched the cold wooden floor. It was nearing the end of the season of Elwah, still some time before the early frosts that would announce the season of Malkizar; the air nevertheless was fresh in the mornings. She wasn't good with the cold. Her hometown was on the plains at the foothills of the Asfaine mountains, near the cave of Gibrar. The weather there was more temperate, the mornings were bright, and the sun would warm the floors. At first, she had missed the courtyards of her house that were filled with plants and the small fountains, the sound of which would fill the dry air with their continuous splashing.

Celeste reached for the large wrap made of wool from the sheep that dot the hills and pastures nestled between the mountains. The shepherds who tend the sheep, also shear them once a year. The women then clean and spin the wool into yarn. She had exchanged this wrap from a young beautiful, vivacious women, named Ulfa who lives in a small village just beyond the forest. All that Ulfa had asked in exchange were some herbs, spices and had pointed to a small porcelain cup painted with summer flowers. Celeste had thought of throwing the cup away as its saucer had broken in the move. Ulfa had smiled broadly at the exchange of the cup.

The wrap was pale cream in colour, soft and warm. Celeste wrapped it around her shoulders relishing the comfort it brought her. She picked up the large comb that her husband had carved from a rare dark wood, a small gift after their marriage. She left the room and made her way to the kitchen. The kitchen was still warm, the fire not quite gone out. Opening the heavy metal door to the wood stove, she cautiously placed a small log on the still smouldering coals. Blowing gently on the coals, she waited for the small flames to lick the log before closing the door. She sat down then and combed her hair, straightening the waves of long dark hair, pulling gently at any knots that had formed during the night.

Celeste picked up a small copper saucepan, filled it with water and placed it on the stove to warm. She opened one jar after another that sat on the shelf, and smelling their content, she finally found the one she wanted. It was the sweet sharp scent of mint she most desired this morning. Replacing the other jars, she took some of the leaves, placing them in a cup to make some tea. Celeste took a long deep breath, settling comfortably on one of the chairs at the table, waiting for the water to boil. She pictured the place she had found the mint growing in a sheltered spot behind their cottage near the first row of trees.

Some time ago, Aïschah had shown her the forest that lay behind her cottage and had introduced her to some of the medicinal herbs she used in her potions. The sunlight that filtered through the canopy of the tall trees, lighting the plants and moss in a random patchwork delighted her. She began to love that forest and its mysteries. And then one day, early in the season of Elwah, Aïschah had taken her to witness the first blooming of the Star flowers, which only appear at the end of the season of Malkizar. Emerging out of the snow in sheltered places in the forest, too shy to grow in the open fields. Celeste was entranced with the delicate flowers, each one a fragile star shape of untainted white and at its centre a small bulb of the purest blue she had ever seen. She had knelt on the damp ground to better appreciate them.

Aïschah knew then for certain that Celeste possessed the sight. Woodland sprites had appeared one after the other around her, celebrating her love and admiration for the flowers. Celeste had simply turned to them, nodded, and smiled. Aïschah made a mental note that if ever Celeste and Haakon were to create an offspring, it would be a very special child that would need careful nurturing.

Celeste closed her eyes reminiscing at the memory of the Star flowers. Without realising it, she relaxed, she drifted as if again experiencing the scent of the pine trees in the early morning sun of that day. Her mind wandered back to the sight of the flowers. *How blue were the centres of those flowers, so blue it reminds me...* with a start, Celeste opened her eyes, the image of the small boy had just surfaced in her mind again. His eyes reminded her of the star flowers. A stirring energy filled her abdomen, her hands folded over her stomach and although she was unsure, a small fear made her shiver. This was the height of the season of Elwah, although the mornings were still cool in the mountains, on the plains of her hometown, the sun would be scorching hot. Celeste made a quick calculation; it must have been in the second mahé of Elwah. *I must see Aïschah without delay to ask her about this,* she thought.

2

Aïschah sat thoughtful, musing over the chart she had just prepared. It was her own star chart, recalculated and drawn again with certain questions in mind. The lines joining certain aspects of the chart were strictly designed to address her recent deliberations on her aspiration, and not least of all, her ability to take on an apprentice; something she had never contemplated but now suddenly, a desire had surfaced, prompted by some unseen force.

Some of the stars aligned perfectly, giving a strong favourable prediction. She frowned slightly at another set of lines linked to the constellation of the Fire beast. It hinted at a death. Aïschah had reviewed her calculations several times.

Aïschah had even re-drawn the chart twice to make sure. The calculations were accurate. The outcome was favourable, the timeline though was considerable. It would take at least eight to twelve years to manifest and twenty years to come to fruition. She sighed, she needed another chart – that of the person or persons that would contribute to this outcome. And yet... there was also this prediction of a death that unsettled her. The line that predicted this, intersected one that linked the evening star. A confirmation of a death but with an easing of suffering.

This will be my life's work, she thought. *Even if it takes twenty years, the outcome is favourable – never assured* she reminded herself, *but favourable. Perhaps if the child is talented... perhaps, it could take less time.* She looked again at the crisscrossing of the lines. *Yes, there was a potential for shortening the outcome...the possibilities were there. It just depends on who it is.* She sighed again. Taking one last look at the chart, she was about to roll it up, when a small detail attracted her attention. She suddenly experienced something like a cold draft of air. Her skin was suddenly covered with goose bumps. There was a small conjunction in the chart. It indicated a secret—a very old, hidden possibility. She stood up, looking at it and stared. No matter how long she stared at it, the conjunction would not reveal itself. It just hinted at something hidden, something important. She sighed again, resolved to examine it again later. She rolled it up, tied it with a piece of red yarn and wrote the date in ink on the outside. She carefully placed it on the shelf with her other parchments.

Aïschah had recently achieved the seventh and final level of Master magician. She now bears the last tattoo mark of having fulfilled the requirements. She has been accepted as an elder on the Council of Elders and Magicians of Naasée. She is now addressed as 'Mahjira'. Her early interest in herbal medicine had led her upon the path of healing and eventually she had developed other skills. A master recognised those skills and instructed her on the art of star gazing and star mapping, marvelling at her aptitude for this. She eventually developed second sight, initially delighting in viewing the world around her that is mostly invisible to ordinary people. She is particularly enchanted with the spirits she sees in the forest. Sometimes shy, they will only reveal themselves if they feel they could be of help in locating the right plant for making healing potions. On very rare occasions, they might issue a warning if an aggressive animal such as a hunting wolf or bear is nearby. The communications are always in images they project to her mind; they never speak with words. She soon realised though that to continue to live in the world, she would need to control her sight and only use it when necessary for healing or finding the right herbs.

The Hills people who live in a small village in a valley beyond the forest, would on occasions seek her out for her medicinal ointments. Generally, though, they would only contact her if she was in the forest. That eventually led to her visiting them, to save on time. They hold her in high regard as a magician and healer. She gives them medicine that she prepares freely. Their pride however obliged them to give something in return. An agreement was made long ago, that in exchange, they would supply her with milk, butter and cheese made from the milk of ewes and goats, and occasionally with sheep skins and wool for the cold months of the year.

The hills people are adept at navigating the forest and even able to ward off wolves. They took it upon themselves to see to her safety without her direct knowledge. There were times when she sensed their presence and always marvelled at their ability to move through the forest without making a sound. They became accustomed to her presence in the forest and often appeared almost without sound to greet her and lead her to a particular bush that is loaded with ripe berries.

Conveniently, with easy access to the forest and all that it holds for making healing potions, Aïschah's cottage is a little outside the main village; it sits high on the side of the hill that borders the line of pine trees that form the first part of the forest. Facing south, it has a view of the Asfaine mountains. In the tradition of most mountain cottages, the construction is simple and made of wooden logs. There is a second floor that comprises of two large bedrooms and a small study, with windows overlooking the slopes that lead to the village.

Adjacent to the main residence, is a smaller cottage that Aïschah occasionally uses for visiting guests.

***

The sun had not even touched the tips of the Asfaine mountains, the sky was only beginning to lighten. Large clouds were gathering. Aïschah walked out of the herbarium and away from the chart's mysteries. It was time to collect some herbs before the heat of the early sunlight spoiled the leaves. Already dressed for a cool morning, she stopped, and walked back to the herbarium, remembering her ceremonial knife; a small silver blade with a wooden handle carved from apple wood. She scoured the main bench where she normally prepares the herbal potions. The knife was nowhere to be seen. A small annoyance began to niggle at her resolve to remain calm. The mystery of the chart and now this. The day was either preparing itself for something irritating or something big. She mused that perhaps— one of the nature spirits, ...*no, they would not be so rude as to dare hide her knife.* Her steel blue eyes scoured the bench, the table and some of the shelves. Taking a deep breath, she was about to surrender and seek another instrument from the kitchen, *but this would not do. The knife is consecrated, it is engraved with sacred runes to protect the plant that is being harvested.*

A small sharp, dry noise behind her brought her out of her tension. Her shoulders relaxed; the sound was familiar. Turning back to the bench, the knife sat there innocently, the early morning light making the blade glint at her in a slightly mocking way.

A small woodland sprite materialised next to the knife. Aïschah raised her left eyebrow in a serious query that would have intimidated the most confident individual. She was about to formulate a rude question in her mind directing it to the sprite. The small nymph looked at her with an apologetic smile. Aïschah then saw the mental picture it sent to her. She saw the knife resting near some bushes in a glade. Aïschah realised that she had inadvertently left the knife there the day before after collecting some interesting specimens. She mentally thanked the woodland spirit for finding and bringing back her small treasure. With a small bow the nymph dematerialised leaving an imperceptible scent of lily of the valley.

Aïschah decided to focus on this morning's harvest and leave the enigma of the star chart for later in the day. Taking her small knife, small pockets made of parchment for storing her collected specimens, she also took a wicker basket for collecting herbs, both medicinal as well as for cooking,

Aïschah stepped out of her kitchen and took twenty steps on the still dewy grass, she was in the forest. The first scent she became aware of was that of the wet moss and the small shrubs that crowded beneath the canopy of the tall trees. As she walked deeper amongst the trees, and the air became noticeably cooler, the fragrance of the old oak trees lay as a soft layer in the air. The scent of the pine trees would only announce itself once the first rays of the sun hit the uppermost branches. Aïschah paused a moment, reflecting on what herbs she needed. No one had come to her with any specific ailments. A strange impulse to seek out raspberries and peppermint grew persistently. Aware that these instincts arose in her for a reason yet to be revealed, she decided to seek out the part of the forest where she knew these grew wild. *There are several uses of these herbs*, she reflected, *they mostly have a soothing effect on the individual. There is something else though,* she thought, *I can't quite put my finger on it.* Trusting, as always for these things to be revealed in their own good time, she continued in her search.

The sun had just risen turning the tips of the mountains to a soft golden hue against a sky of cornflower blue. It would be several hours before the light would reach through the canopy and illuminate the smaller shrubs and herbs of the forest. She still had time. She reached the clearing and found what she was looking for, nestled around an outcrop of rocks, and growing in the shade of one of the old trees, the peppermint was doing exceptionally well, thriving with the moisture of the moss that covered the tops of the rocks and positioned well enough to receive a few hours of direct sunlight.

The raspberry bush grew a little apart and closer to the centre of the clearing, where it would benefit from several hours of direct sunlight. The tall trees around it protected it from the strong winds and frost. She had just cut several samples of leaves from both, when a sensation informed her that a presence was nearby. She paused waiting for a confirmation.

The sound of a breaking twig behind her announced the presence. She did not sense any danger and so turned around slowly. A young man stood on the edge of the clearing, smiling at her. It was a young man from the Hills people. She understood that the breaking of the twig was his way of announcing himself. He would otherwise not have made a single sound.

Aïschah smiled at him, recognising one of the shepherds. He bowed to her and approached, looking at the leaves she had just collected.

"Mistress Aïschah," he began.

"Errai." She referred to his name, with a slight questioning look, meaning to confirm that her memory of him was correct. His, was a name from his father's side, who came from a tribe in the Great Desert of Keyab. His name literally translates to 'shepherd'.

He smiled back in acknowledgement, pleased that she had recognised him.

He then approached her with a degree of caution that deferred to her reputation as healer and magician.

"Mistress, I have been sent to seek you out. One of our women, Ulfa, is not feeling well and asks for your help."

"I will follow you Errai. I have what I need."

They set out, Errai leading with his accustomed long strides. Aïschah had no difficulty in keeping up with him. She smelled the fragrance of the village wood fires as the sun rose to the top of the trees. Within moments they reached the village; it lay open, nestled between two sides of the mountain.

Ulfa's house was the first one on this side of the village. It was a simple affair as all the village of shepherds' houses were. Made from local wood and thatched rooves. Most only had one large room that functioned as meals and sleeping. While tending their sheep, the younger shepherds would not return home, they often slept in small stone huts, strategically constructed on the farthest hills. They served as shelter during inclement weather.

Some larger families could boast to have two rooms, one for sleeping and the other for meals and receiving guests. Ulfa was still a young woman and only recently married. The house was small. Aïschah entered taking note of the interior. A window at the far end barely lit the room. A piece of clean material acting as a makeshift curtain, was pulled to one side to let the light in. The material is embroidered with a distinct edge of humble flowers. The room was simply furnished; a table and two stools for meals; a set of shelves roughly hewn out of hard wood was set against a wall with wooden cups and plates for everyday use. In the centre of the shelf, a single beautiful porcelain cup painted with summer flowers took pride of place.

Against one wall, a small wood stove was lit to heat the house as well as providing a means to cook the meals. Woodsmoke from this morning's fire still permeated the air.

Ulfa was sitting on the edge of a cot bed. Aïschah took one look at her pale complexion and judging from the slight sour smell in the air, knew that she had not been able to hold any food down.

"Ulfa, where is your husband?"

Ulfa's weary eyes were slightly unfocussed, her shoulders slumped slightly at the question.

"He left a few weeks ago to hunt the large white bears with his father's tribe in the far north regions." Almost in way to justify his absence, she added, "The hunting has been poor this year. His people are having a hard time feeding themselves."

Aïschah nodded in understanding. She took a seat next to Ulfa and taking her hand in hers, felt for her pulse, all the while looking at her Hala, which radiated with intense white strands of light. It didn't take long for Aïschah to realise why she felt the compulsion to bring the herbs that she did.

"Ulfa, you are with child." This was said as a statement and not a question. Nevertheless, Ulfa stared at Aïschah in disbelief.

"How is that possible..." she began, and then stopped. Aïschah could see the mental calculation Ulfa was making. Finally, with a sigh Ulfa looked down at her belly, lifted her eyes to Aïschah and with a slightly forced smile she nodded. "Yes. I think that would explain the nausea." Then with another breath she added, "This is our first child."

There was a note of concern in Ulfa's voice. Aïschah smiled at her, still holding her hand she declared, "All will be well Ulfa. Your child will be healthy and strong and so will you."

Ulfa's eyes moistened with tears. She smiled and whispered, "Thank you, Mistress Aïschah."

Remembering the chart she had drawn earlier, Aïschah could not help but wonder what role would this child play in the future. She pushed that thought aside and focussed on making a tea out of the raspberry leaves to ease Ulfa's nausea. Hesitating for a moment, Aïschah poured the tea in the beautiful porcelain cup, the only porcelain cup in the house, the one that was decorated with summer flowers. Ulfa looked up in surprise, smiling shyly at the cup that would only be used for special occasions. Reading Ulfa's mind, Aïschah smiled and said, "Here Ulfa, this is a special occasion. The tea will help ease your discomfort." And then an intuition came to her as she added, "I sense that you child will be a child of the forest. I also sense that he will play an important role one day." Aïschah had hesitated briefly at the last statement; it was only later she realised that she had said 'he'; a heaviness had weighed upon her with those last words.

She pushed that feeling aside and smiled at Ulfa.

With instructions on how to prepare the tea with the remainder of the raspberry leaves, how often to take it and when to take the peppermint tea, Aïschah left, her mind a little occupied with what she had just experienced. Slowly she made her way back to her cottage, letting the afternoon sunlight warm her and allow the still fresh air of the forest to clear her mind. She could not help herself though, making a quick calculation, she estimated that Ulfa's child would be born sometime at the beginning the next season of Malkizar. *A child of the northern star,* she mused to herself, *A being of guidance and protection for the traveller,* quoting the old parchment titled: *The Language of the Stars* and the chronology of births listed therein.

3

❧

The forest trees thinned out, the well-trodden path that led out of the forest meandered and finally around a curve, she could see her cottage. She stopped. A figure was crouched on the back step, just outside her kitchen door. From this distance she could not make out who it was. She focussed her energy outward to the person that was stooped over and searched her instincts; there was no danger.

Nearing the cottage, she recognised with a slight shock the outline of a woman. Celeste was sitting on the step, her head resting into her arms folded over her knees. She wore a large cream coloured shawl. Probably sensing a presence, Celeste looked up suddenly and then smiled, recognising Aïschah.

She looks tired, Aïschah thought, *something is weighing on her mind.* Aïschah knew that Celeste's husband was not keen on her visiting her cottage. For all the strength of character Haakon had, he was still biased against what he called the 'old ways', mostly referring to the superstitions that people have regarding magic.

A small shudder of anticipation coursed through her body. *This will indeed be a day unlike any other,* Aïschah mused, *first the chart, Ulfa's pregnancy and now this. I can hardly wait to hear what is on Celeste's mind.*

Aïschah stepped forward to the back entrance smiling at Celeste.

Not strictly intruding into Celeste's mind, Aïschah nevertheless used her sight to take a glimpse at her Hala. The energy was buoyant emanating in all directions, but for some reason, there seemed to be a shield preventing Aïschah from delving further. Aïschah smiled back and reaching Celeste, folded her into a warm embrace.

"You are here very early, Celeste." Aïschah looked into her eyes. Years ago, upon their first meeting, she had noted that Celeste's eyes were unusually blue; the more so because her tribe came from the Desert of Keyab, where such colouring was unusual and quiet often associated with deep magic. Today though, there was an extra sparkle in Celeste's eye, almost as if the blue had intensified overnight.

Celeste gave her a slightly impish smile, "I knew *you* would be up early collecting your herbs." Peering into Aïschah's basket, she added, "but obviously not early enough to catch up to you."

Aïschah nodded, "I took some medicine to a woman in the Hills village;" responding to Celeste's sudden expression of concern, adding, "Nothing serious. She is well."

They went inside and Aïschah prepared some tea. On impulse she used the fresh peppermint leaves she had just collected, only realising moments later that she had done so without premeditated thought. She smiled to herself, her curiosity of what lay on Celeste's mind deepening.

Celeste sat at the table, an ease of gesture indicating her level of comfort with Aïschah. She was looking down at her hands, her fingers interlaced, almost in a sign of supplication. Her fingers elegant and long, an indication of deep feelings, bordering on heightened sensitivity and spirituality.

Aïschah poured the tea into two cups and presented Celeste with a jar of honey, to which Celeste shook her head in negation. Celeste carefully brought the cup to her lip, blowing a little, releasing a small cloud of steam and took a sip. She placed her cup back down on the table, her head still bowed slightly. Aïschah waited, knowing that she could not rush the situation.

Finally, Celeste took a breath, raising her head, she looked directly into Aïschah's eyes and began, "I had a dream that both disturbs and entrances me." Aïschah waited. "This," she sighed, "this is the third time I have dreamed this and each time it affects me deeply." She looked down briefly at her hands before continuing, "I know that you regard something that happens three times as particularly important."

Aïschah smiled, wanting to encourage her without disrupting the obvious energy that still hung over the memory of Celeste's dream.

"It begins always with a vastness of blue, it is a large ocean. I feel a sense of calm and awe at the limitlessness of it. Just as I think that it is the end of the dream, the face of a small boy emerges from the water. He has stark black hair and blue eyes that remind me of the Star flowers. As I wonder about the name of the ocean, a small voice tells me that it is the Ocean of Malkizar. The boy then looks directly at me and smiles such a radiant smile that it melts my heart."

Celeste looked up, tears welling in her eyes.

The hairs on the back of Aïschah's neck rose and her whole being became watchful; the room was suddenly filled with the tense energy of lightning during a summer storm before it explodes. A wave of alertness coursed through Aïschah's whole body. Her back straightened, her gaze became unfocussed and distant. For a moment, she was speechless, staring beyond Celeste. Her mind now divided between what Celeste had just told her and the chart she had but drawn this morning.

"Aïschah?" Celeste looked concerned.

Aïschah shook her head slightly, bringing her focus back to the room and Celeste.

"Aïschah? Is this a bad omen?"

Aïschah was silent for a moment, not knowing where to begin. She realised that Celeste was now becoming anxious.

"No. No, Celeste, this is not a bad omen." With as little emotion in her voice, she added, "Celeste, tell me, when was your last cycle?"

Celeste looked puzzled for a moment, uncertain at the change of topic. Without thinking about it too much, she replied, "About a mahé..." Her facial composure dropped, and she added, "Oh."

Another wave of prickling energy coursed through Aïschah's body.

A silence like glass hung over Aïschah's kitchen.

Celeste did not want to say it. To articulate what suddenly came to her mind was overwhelming.

Aïschah took a breath, poured tea for them both. Placing the pot back carefully, she sat opposite Celeste and smiled.

"I think the dream you had is a revelation. A prediction if you will. I think that you are either with child or soon to be. The child is calling out to you, greeting you in the best way it can. There is no doubt in my mind that he is expressing love to you."

The focus in Aïschah's eyes again softened and almost as a whisper, she added, "I am certain that you will give birth to a boy. Whether he will have black hair and blue eyes, remains to be seen. But the symbols of the ocean Malkizar and the abundance of the colour blue, signify to me that the child will be born during the season of Malkizar. He will be a twilight child, born between the waters and the light of the world." She paused; Celeste was visibly moved. "I cannot say more at this point Celeste. I will need to consult your stars as well as the child's."

Looking at the basket filled with peppermint and raspberry leaves, Aïschah smiled inwardly, realising now, that the impulse to collect those herbs were equally meant for Ulfa as well as Celeste. She pushed the basket toward Celeste, "You will find these helpful in the coming months. They will ease any nausea you may experience and strengthen your body for nourishing the child within you."

Celeste's face was pale. This was not the news she had prepared herself for. She unfolded her hands and brought them to rest on her lap, shielding her stomach.

"Celeste, how do you feel?" Aïschah filled her voice with as much calm and kindness as she could.

Celeste looked up, gave Aïschah a weak smile, "I," she began hesitatingly, "I am not sure." Releasing her breath slowly, she added, "I was not sure what the dream meant, but now that you explain it, it makes sense. Of course, I am excited to be able to bear a child. To think that this child is as beautiful as the one I saw in my dreams, my heart if filled with joy."

Celeste paused. Aïschah saw the uncertainty. It had to do with Haakon, her husband.

"Have you thought how you will tell Haakon?"

Celeste's brow furrowed with a momentary thought.

"I will tell him, of course. I know he will be pleased; we had discussed having a child some time ago."

Aïschah heard a 'but' in that last remark. She waited for Celeste to express it. Hesitantly, she began, "I do not think I should tell him about the dream or your interpretation." Celeste paused, letting out a sigh, "He will only see it as magic. I think it is better if I tell him that my cycle has stopped and that this is what I suspect. He will see soon enough as the child grows within me."

Aïschah nodded, a part of her understood, yet another tightened at the thought of the denial of her skill as a healer and seer. With an internal breath she released the conflict in her mind.

Celeste stood up smiling, "Aïschah, thank you. May I take some of these herbs with me?"

"Yes, yes of course, they are meant for you."

Celeste looked in awe and then checked herself; of course, Aïschah would have known.

"Those are peppermint, and those? Are they raspberry leaves?"

"Yes Celeste, they are. Both will help with the nausea and be of a calming influence."

"Thank you, Aïschah."

Aïschah could see that she had another unspoken question.

"Celeste, I assure you, your child will be healthy and well." She did not add what she thought of his future. She would need to check the star chart and the Chronicles of star dates.

Celeste left with a look of hope, a timid smile, and a whispered, "Thank you."

Aïschah stood looking out of the southern window, watching Celeste walk off with a lighter step. Her gaze wandered down to the village, she briefly wondered at how well Haakon would take the news.

She shook herself back to the present and immediately went into the herbarium where she pulled out the chart, unrolled it and weighed the corners with jars of herbs that still had to be labelled.

Aïschah made some quick adjustments based on her calculations of Celeste's estimated date of conception. She looked at the chart over and over. She again checked the additional lines and designs. For the first time in a long time, Aïschah experienced a turmoil within. Too many possibilities were presenting themselves. And then, there was that conjunction, the one that hinted as something hidden. Each time she looked at it, she was overwhelmed with wonder. Her skin crawled with goosebumps. Energy constantly ran up and down her body.

A thought kept repeating itself in her mind, no matter how often she tried to dismiss it, it would restate itself with greater urgency. The thought was that she should immediately check the book of ancient prophecies. Specifically, the prophecy regarding the Sacred Tears of Apphat.

She tried in vain to speak to that thought, *it is not possible! The mother is untrained. This is simply my own hidden agenda. My desire!* She spoke to it strongly in her mind, saying *No, I refuse to believe that this is so.* The conflict rose beyond her control. In the end, she thought she would consult another mage. *But who? Who is without their own agenda and who would be able to know for certain?* Then a name surfaced, *Elwah. Elwah Tahir, Haafiz of the sacred Tear of Naasée.* But then, the Tears of Apphat had not been seen in a hundred years. No one knew for sure if the Tears had been safeguarded after King Apphat's death, and if so, no one knew for certain where they were. Just to say that Elwah Tahir was one of the Sacred Haafiz – Keeper of one of the sapphires, was not conclusive proof that he actually held it. His title may simply have implied that at one point, as the history books recorded it, the High Priests of Naasée had successfully saved and guarded one of the Tears.

Elwah Tahir is the prince of Naasée; high priest and ruler of the Council of Elders and magicians in Naasée. He is regarded as a highly powerful magician and seer. His powers are renowned throughout the four kingdoms. Although he appears to be in his late thirties, his age is indeterminate, common consensus is that he is at least a hundred years old.

Aïschah resolved to contact Elwah.

4

Aïschah looked around at the herbarium, taking stock of the jars of herbs and flowers. Everything was in its place, and there was a place for everything. She took great pride in making sure that anything in her herbarium could be found. There was a logic to it. Her recent experience of the misplaced knife irritated her. It was so unlike her to be so distracted. The herbarium is as much her workspace as her sanctuary. No one was allowed in without permission.

It was nearing the end of the season of Elwah. Flowers in the fields were still in full bloom. She was well stocked with herbal remedies. It would not be long before the hazelnut matured and were ready for collection; that is of course if the squirrels did not eat most of them. *The leaves will soon turn in colour,* she thought. It will then be time to collect barks from certain trees, and the moss that should be kept moist, if possible, to use to dress wounds.

Like bees around a honey hive, too many things were pressing in her head. Aïschah decided to take a walk in the forest, for no other reason than to try and clear her mind. If she is to contact prince Elwah, the high priest of Naasée, she would need to have all her facts sorted.

From the kitchen door, the twenty steps that it took for Aïschah to reach the edge of the forest, she could feel her shoulders relax, her back straighten. Taking deep long breaths, her body began to yield to the warm early afternoon sun. The fragrance of flowers mixed with the deep notes of moss and trees, filled her with a pleasing sense of peace. She didn't take her little silver knife with her. She purposely left it behind, there would be no work, no collection of medicinal herbs on this outing. This would just be for the pleasure of connecting with the forest. She thought about the last time she took that pleasure and surprised herself that it had been so long. Smiling to herself, Aïschah felt her step lighten, her breaths deepening and her cares melting away.

The occasional twittering of birds echoed through the forest. A single loud bird call, indignant at her intrusion was repeated by its mate deeper in the forest. It was as if they were relaying her whereabouts. A gentle wind whispered in the tops of the trees. Large shrubs still green from their summer flush of leaves, stood out in the dappled light that streamed through the canopy. Insects dancing in the beams of light were mixed with occasional small clouds of pollen. Her steps were muffled on the still damp earth and decaying branches. Occasionally a stray twig snaped underfoot. Aïschah lost in the wonder of the forest, noticed a little used path turn off the main track; with an idle curiosity she decided to follow it a while and see where it led.

A large tree lay partially across the path, fallen in the last storm. Its roots exposed to the air, the soil around it already filling up with ferns and mushrooms. She made a mental note to come back later and collect some of these. Carefully negotiating around the larger branches, she managed to avoid getting her woollen top getting caught. With a sense of victory and agility at escaping the clutches of the dying tree, she turned allowing herself a superior triumphant smile at the fallen tree. The smile was quickly erased as she stumbled on an exposed root across the path, almost forcing an expletive from her. Regaining control, she reminded herself to be more careful and patient with nature; after all it was not the tree's fault. Amused at her own pride and quick temper, she wondered how she would cope teaching a young apprentice.

The path's surface became irregular, there were obvious signs of water having washed away some of the soil exposing rocks and tree roots. She paused, looking for a tall straight piece of wood that she could use to stabilise her steps. A large branch near a sturdy oak tree, was half hidden amongst the undergrowth. She pulled it out. It was smooth and perfect both in height and strength. Leaning on her new-found friend, she noticed that the path was beginning to drop off sharply. Her curiosity heightened, she determined to find where this path ran.

It was not long before she heard the murmur of running water. Excitement filled her. She loved water, always refreshing on a hot summer's day; the water coming down from the top of the mountain would no doubt be freezing cold. She shivered at the thought but eager to see this source of water so close to her cottage.

Some of the undergrowth had thickened, obviously taking advantage of the abundant supply of water and nutrients from the forest floor above. A little further down, a few tall trees seemed to form a circular curtain. The path took a sharp curve and seemed to stop near a large flat rock. A moment later, she was glad to have slowed down. Upon reaching the rock, she realised that she was standing above a large pool of water. The rock was poised in mid-air above the water. To the right of it, a small stream ended in a waterfall and was feeding the pond in a continuous gurgle of splashing sounds.

A sharp memory pulled at her heart. She remembered another pool, another time, long ago. His arm around her shoulders, both of their feet dangling in the cool water, and both laughing light-heartedly. He had been so excited to show her his secret discovery. Aïschah paused, taken by the sudden emotion she had not experienced in decades. Her heartbeat noticeably beating loudly in her chest, moisture in her eyes, *This is silly,* she thought. Nevertheless, she allowed the fullness of the memory to fill her; a slight sadness arising from deep within her. She wiped her eyes gently and looked down at the water. Making the decision to see if she could find a way down to the water's edge, she now wanted to dangle her feet in this water and rest a while.

She eased her way down and found a large flat rock that sat right on the edge of the deepest part of the water. It was perfect for sitting and at the right height that only her feet and ankles would be in the water. She eased herself onto the rock and removed her shoes, being careful to place them behind her so that they would not accidentally fall into the water. She then removed her thick woollen socks, the pattern of the knitted socks leaving a slight imprint on her white feet. Her feet felt hot and sweaty, she looked forward to dipping them into the cool mountain water. Tentatively, she dipped just a toe into the water, and then her whole foot. She gasped at the icy feel of it, tempted to draw it back. The coolness was sweet and inviting. She braced herself and at once plunged the other foot in the water, a blunt bite against her white skin.

She relaxed then, allowing the sweetness of the cold water turning the skin of her white feet into slightly pink socks from the blood rushing in to try and warm her up again. She smiled aware of the tension in her body and allowed her shoulders to loosen.

Her mind wandered back to the herbarium and to the chart. She thought again of the hidden conjunction and the hint of something to do with a prophecy written a long time ago. She was sure that she had made a copy of the sacred parchment. She would look for it and re-read it. Quite unexpectedly, a small voice spoke in the back of her mind, *"Even if you read it again, you will not understand it. It was written in code a long time ago, to confound even the cleverest of them all."*

Aïschah sat up straight, surprised by the voice she just heard.

She relaxed once more, allowing her sight to soften. She would try to access more information by using her second sight. Without warning and surprisingly without effort on her part, a light seemed to suddenly spread across the surface of the pond.

The water shimmered, an expanse of blue washed across the still surface and image after image rose seemingly from the depth.

She saw the boy that Celeste had seen in her dreams. He smiled at her also. Many faces also appeared, and unclear events that sped past. A voice spoke then, grave, and slow,

"For only he can speak the true name of the King, for the king has two names. They are the names of the incantation that will heal the world. One will guide and protect him to the end of his days, for they were both born of the waters of creation. Though he is born of the Tears of Sorrow, and will suffer for it, another will love him, who will gift him with the Tear of Joy. And yet a third, who will become one with him, though he holds the balance of destiny to heal the world, also holds the power to destroy it. It is only in their unity that the incantation may be sung, and thereby restore the Great Harmony. This is the prophecy. Many have sought to understand it, few have been given the revelation. Guard it and treasure it."

The sunlight on the still water suddenly intense, momentarily blinded her and the wondrous images vanished as if made of mist.

Aïschah sat very still. She could no longer feel the cold of the water. Instead, a gentle warmth filled her entire being as she used her skill to memorise every word that had just been spoken. Although the words were simple enough, the content was enigmatic. As with most prophecies, there were no clear links to existing persons and no clear narrative. The true significance was always shrouded in mystery, like a puzzle not easily solved. Slowly as if waking from a pleasant dream, her focus came back to the pool and the forest around her. A strand of sunlight penetrated through the canopy above and warmed her back.

She removed her feet from the cool mountain water and let them dry a little before putting on her socks and shoes. She noticed how much her feet had shrunk with the cold water and how easily they now slipped into her shoes. She sat there a little while longer, soaking in the sweetness of the peace. She got up then, and making a commitment to come here often, she set back onto the path to her cottage, with the firm intention of carefully revising her star chart before contacting Prince Elwah.

The walk back, was less strenuous than the earlier climb. The small aches in her legs and back from the exercise gave her a satisfying sense of physical accomplishment. Her mind had cleared of previous concerns. By the time she got back to her cottage, the sun was setting behind the mountains, turning the sky a cerulean blue, the air cooled quickly. *I will have a warm soaking bath before attempting anything else*, she thought.

She went into the kitchen first, making sure that the stove was alight and hot. She fed it a few more pieces of wood, just in case. There was a dull metal pipe that twisted and snaked behind the stove, heating water that came from a large rainwater reservoir at the back of the cottage. Back in the bathroom, she turned the tap on and waited. Moments passed and the water began to fill the tub with warm water. As an afterthought, she decided to put in some herbs. *Something to soothe, but not relax me so much that I would want to fall asleep.* The irony made her smile, there were still plenty of peppermint leaves in her basket from this morning's collection. Peppermint would soothe away any aches, melt away any mental stress and keep her fresh and alert.

Steam was building up inside the bathroom, droplets were starting to bead on the solid pinewood walls. She sat a while on the edge of the bath waiting for the right amount of water. She turned off the tap, and took off her hiking clothes, hanging them on a wooden peg behind the door. She shivered a little. Gathering her wiry light-coloured hair that could never be tamed, she bound it with a small strip of white cotton cloth. One arm across her chest, the other to support herself, she tentatively tested the water with a toe. She pulled it out a little, the water was very warm against her cool skin. She smiled at the feel of it. She plunged one foot and then the other, taking in a quick breath at the shock of the heat. Then she lowered herself, both hands now on the edge of the tub for balance, and with one decisive movement, she eased the rest of her body in the warm water. The worst of the hot prickling sensation on her skin over, she relaxed and closed her eyes, letting out a long satisfying breath. The fragrance of peppermint surrounding her like a cloud of mountain freshness.

***

Early evening darkened the herbarium with the light of dusk, filling the recesses with shadows. A stray beam of orange light accenting a shelf, quickly faded. Fresh from her bath, Aïschah lit some oil lamps, and placed another piece of apple wood in the small wood-stove to warm the place a little. She looked at the chart once more. It did not reveal anything more. If anything, it created more mystery. More questions arose.

She pulled out a small bag of pebbles that had each been painted with ancient runes. She felt a little awkward at having to rely on this ancient way of divining and not wholly trusting her own instincts. *I just need a confirmation,* she thought. Her fingers found a stone, she pulled out one rune and looked at it. The rune of *Raido* stared back at her. It was cautioning not to force a decision, but to allow the power of destiny to flow. She had asked whether contacting Elwah was such a good idea after all. She did not need any more confirmation to her instinct. She put the stone back in the pouch and resolved to wait until after Celeste's child was born. She would revisit that question then. She remembered the vision and the voice she had experienced by the pond in the mountain early that afternoon. Although she could mostly guess the date, the precision of the actual date of birth would be best.

5

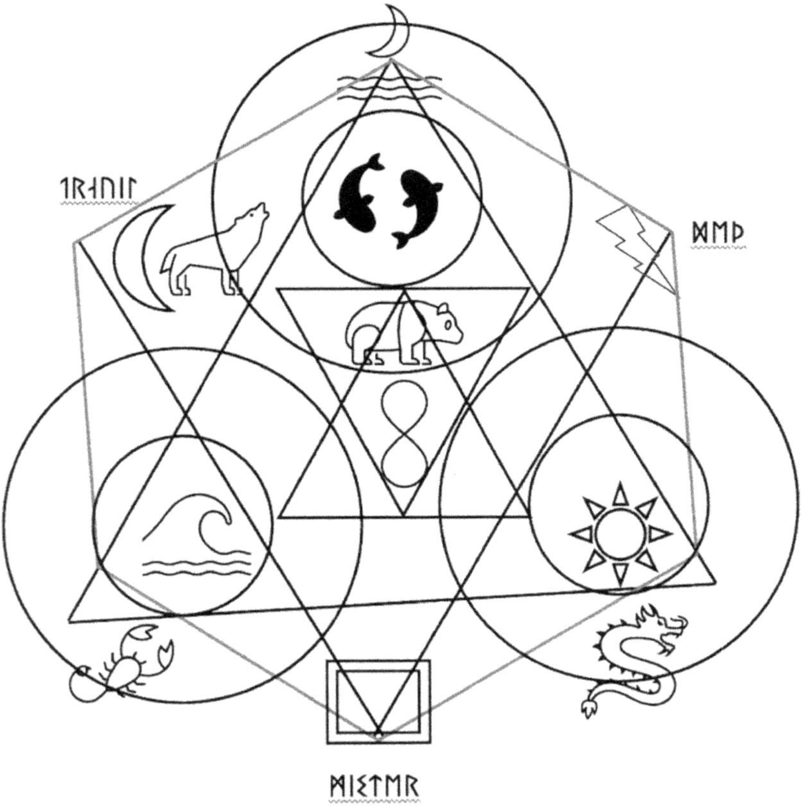

Novels by Alain Louis Camus

The Chronicles of Azizi series:

2023 - The Tears of Apphat - Immortal Beloved
2024 - Aïschah - Silver Moon. Language of the Stars
          A companion novella to The Tears of Apphat.
 - Silence of the Stars - Book 2 of The Chronicle of Azizi. Publication *date
to be announced*

www.ingramcontent.com/pod-product-compliance
Lightning Source LLC
Chambersburg PA
CBHW042035120726
47911CB00027B/745